Dear Parent:

Congratulations! Your child is taking the first steps on an exciting journey. The destination? Independent reading!

STEP INTO READING® will help your child get there. The program offers five steps to reading success. Each step includes fun stories and colorful art. There are also Step into Reading Sticker Books, Step into Reading Math Readers, Step into Reading Phonics Readers, Step into Reading Write-In Readers, and Step into Reading Phonics Boxed Sets—a complete literacy program with something to interest every child.

Learning to Read, Step by Step!

Ready to Read   Preschool–Kindergarten
• big type and easy words • rhyme and rhythm • picture clues
For children who know the alphabet and are eager to begin reading.

Reading with Help   Preschool–Grade 1
• basic vocabulary • short sentences • simple stories
For children who recognize familiar words and sound out new words with help.

Reading on Your Own   Grades 1–3
• engaging characters • easy-to-follow plots • popular topics
For children who are ready to read on their own.

Reading Paragraphs   Grades 2–3
• challenging vocabulary • short paragraphs • exciting stories
For newly independent readers who read simple sentences with confidence.

Ready for Chapters   Grades 2–4
• chapters • longer paragraphs • full-color art
For children who want to take the plunge into chapter books but still like colorful pictures.

STEP INTO READING® is designed to give every child a successful reading experience. The grade levels are only guides. Children can progress through the steps at their own speed, developing confidence in their reading, no matter what their grade.

Remember, a lifetime love of reading starts with a single step!

Visit us on the Web!
StepIntoReading.com
randomhouse.com/kids

Educators and librarians, for a variety of teaching tools, visit us at RHTeachersLibrarians.com

ISBN 978-0-385-36974-9 (trade) — ISBN 978-0-385-36975-6 (lib. bdg.)
Printed in the United States of America
10 9 8 7 6 5 4 3 2

GIDDY-UP, GUPPIES!

By Josephine Nagaraj

Based on the teleplay "The Cowgirl Parade!"
by Emmy Laybourne

Cover illustrated by Sue DiCicco and Steve Talkowski
Interior illustrated by John Huxtable

Random House 🏠 New York

Howdy!
Look.
Cowgirl Dusty
rides into town.

She rides
her horse, Rusty.
Giddy-up!

Cowgirl Dusty ropes
a young calf
with her lasso.

A lasso is
a loop of rope.
Cowboys and cowgirls
twirl lassos.

Molly wants
to be a cowgirl.
She wears
a cowgirl hat.

She puts on
a cowgirl vest.

She rides
a horse.

She does tricks
with her lasso!

It is fun to be

a cowboy

or a cowgirl!

Molly and her friends
twirl their lassos.
They do
a lasso dance!

The cowgirl parade
is today.
The sun is shining.

Balloons float.

It is a party!

Yee-haw!

A marching band plays.
The bandleader
twirls his baton.

Music fills the air.

Everyone dances!

Cowgirls ride in
on their horses.
They wave flags.

The crowd claps
and cheers.

Cows follow
the cowgirls.

Look!

A baby calf.

<u>Moo!</u>

Cowgirl Dusty
rides in on Rusty.
She twirls her lasso.

A balloon pops.

BANG!

The sound scares
the calf.

Oh, no!
The calf
runs away!
Who will
catch the calf?

Molly knows
what to do.

She climbs
onto Rusty.
Giddy-up!

Molly twirls
her lasso
like a real cowgirl.

She ropes

the calf!

The crowd roars!
Molly is the hero
of the cowgirl parade!

Yee-haw!

Giddy-up, Guppies!